NANCY DREW
#12 DREW girl detective ®

Dress Reversal

STEFAN PETRUCHA & SARAH KINNEY • Writers
SHO MURASE • Artist
with 3D CG elements and color by CARLOS JOSE GUZMAN
Based on the series by
CAROLYN KEENE

New York

Dress Reversal
STEFAN PETRUCHA & SARAH KINNEY – Writers
SHO MURASE – Artist
with 3D CG elements and color by CARLOS JOSE GUZMAN
BRYAN SENKA – Letterer
JOHN McCARTHY – Production
JIM SALICRUP
Editor-in-Chief

ISBN 10: 1-59707-086-6 paperback edition
ISBN 13: 978-1-59707-086-7 paperback edition
ISBN 10: 1-59707-087-4 hardcover edition
ISBN 13: 978-1-59707-087-4 hardcover edition

6-11-09

Printed in China.
Distributed by Macmillan.

10   9   8   7   6   5   4   3   2   1

=SIGH=
I SURE DON'T WANT TO SPEND THE WHOLE DAY IN THIS LITTLE ROOM.

FASHION IS ABOUT PATIENCE AND PERSEVERANCE! *PERFECT* DOESN'T HAPPEN ON THE FIRST TRY, MISSY.

LOOKS FINE TO ME.

FINE? YOU LOOK... *PERFECT!*

YOU JUST GOT LUCKY, NANCE.

POOR BESS, WHO'S ALWAYS IMPECCABLY DRESSED WITHOUT EVEN TRYING, WAS HAVING A REAL FASHION CRISIS.

AS FOR ME, I WAS FINDING THIS DRESSING ROOM CONVENTION PRETTY DULL. MY ATTENTION KEPT DRIFTING OUT THE DOOR.

LUCKY. YEAH. I GUESS.

ZHIPPP

SO, GEORGE, ARE WE DONE HERE?

YUP! ALL SET. AT LEAST I'LL LOOK GOOD ON THE OUTSIDE WHILE HAVING UGLY THOUGHTS ABOUT DEEDEE INSIDE!

÷SIGH÷ NANCY'S DRESS IS TO DIE FOR, BUT, I'M STILL O FOR THREE! THIS ISN'T SUPPOSED TO HAPPEN!

BUT THE PARTY ITSELF WAS SOMETHING EVEN GEORGE WOULDN'T AVOID, EVEN IF IT WAS AT DEIRDRE'S HOUSE.

SLOW DOWN! DIDN'T YOU EVER HEAR ABOUT BEING FASHIONABLY LATE?! I THOUGHT YOU DIDN'T EVEN WANT TO COME!

YEAH, BUT I LIKE TO SEE PEOPLE ARRIVE.

I JUST LOVE THAT UNCOMFORTABLE LOOK THEY GET AT THE DOOR WHILE THEY LOOK AROUND FOR PEOPLE THEY KNOW AND WONDER WHO'S LOOKING AT THEM.

OKAY, SO YOU'RE JUST *WEIRD!*

YEAH, ISN'T IT GREAT? MAYBE SHE'S SICK OR SOMETHING.

BUT WHAT'S THE POINT OF WEARING DESIGNER DRESSES IF WE CAN'T EMBARRASS DEIRDRE?

OH. YEAH.

THERE SHE IS.

GEE, NOW I DON'T KNOW HOW TO FEEL. DISAPPOINTED THAT SHE'S HERE, OR HAPPY WE CAN SHOW HER UP?

OH, MY GOD! THEY'RE WEARING THE **SAME DRESS!**

OH? I DIDN'T NOTICE.

I NEVER REALLY UNDERSTOOD WHAT THE BIG DEAL ABOUT WEARING THE SAME CLOTHES AS SOMEONE ELSE WAS. THEN AGAIN, I DO WEAR DIFFERENT SOCKS SOMETIMES.

ARE YOU ALL RIGHT?

OHHH! HOW, HOW, COULD YOU?

DEIRDRE SEEMED TO UNDERSTAND EXACTLY WHAT THE PROBLEM WAS, THOUGH.

BETTER CALL AN UNDERTAKER! TURNS OUT THAT DRESS **REALLY IS** TO DIE FOR!

CHAPTER TWO:
WASH AND WHERE?

SHE'S GONE! SHE'S TOTALLY GONE!

YEAH, OUR MYSTERY-SOLVER'S PART OF A MYSTERY HERSELF!

C'MON, WE'VE GOT TO GET HELP!

MEANWHILE, OUR BELOVED RIVER HEIGHTS' POLICE CHIEF McGINNIS WAS FEELING LIKE A FISH OUT OF UNIFORM IN HIS FANCY DUDS.

EMERGENCY! 911! HELP!

OH, DEAR.

UPSET THOUGH THEY WERE, BY THE TIME A PATROLMAN AND MY FATHER ARRIVED, BESS AND GEORGE MANAGED TO GET OUT THE IMPORTANT DETAILS.

DON'T WORRY. WE'LL FIND HER. I'VE GOT AN APB* ON THE VAN YOU DESCRIBED.

DON'T WORRY? HOW CAN WE NOT?

* APB: ALL POINTS BULLETIN.

WHO WOULD KIDNAP NANCY?

MAYBE MORE IMPORTANTLY, WHY?

MEANWHILE, WHILE I MAY HAVE BEEN *OBSESSING*, FOR A CHANGE MY CLOTHES DID *MATCH*, EXCEPT MAYBE FOR THE SACK OVER MY HEAD.

VROOOM!

MOSTLY, THOUGH, I WAS TRYING TO STEADY MYSELF...

...EMOTIONALLY...

...AND *PHYSICALLY*,...

WHUNK!

...WHILE THE VAN DROVE THROUGH EVERY POTHOLE IN TOWN.

OOOMP!

I WAS SO RATTLED, IT TOOK ME A FEW MINUTES TO COLLECT MYSELF ENOUGH TO REALIZE THAT SINCE MY HANDS WERE FREE...

...I COULD TAKE *OFF* THE HOOD.

NOT THAT IT DID MUCH GOOD.

THE INSIDE OF THE VAN WASN'T MUCH MORE INTERESTING THAN THE INSIDE OF THE HOOD.

IT FIGURED THERE WAS NO DOOR HANDLE ON THE INSIDE, THIS WAS A KIDNAPPING, AFTER ALL.

BUT THERE WAS A HOLE, PROBABLY WITH A LOCK INSIDE. IF I HAD SOMETHING TO STICK IN THERE, I MIGHT BE ABLE TO TRIP IT, SOMETHING LIKE A SHOE *HEEL*.

WHAT A TIME TO WEAR FLAT, SENSIBLE SHOES. IT WAS THE FIRST TIME IN MY LIFE I WISHED I'D WORN SPIKED HEELS.

THERE WAS, FOR INSTANCE, THE RICH ENTREPRENEUR I HELPED SEND TO JAIL FOR TWENTY YEARS.

THEN THERE WAS THE SENIOR VICE PRESIDENT I'D GOTTEN FIRED FOR SABOTAGING A BIG PROJECT.

AND THE WOMAN THAT I PROVED WAS A MAN.

AND THE CRAZY WATCHMAN I DRAGGED FROM HIS ONLY HOME!

IT TURNED OUT I COULD EVEN *SHORTEN* THE LIST BY ASKING WHO *WOULDN'T* WANT TO KIDNAP ME?

SO, CLEARLY, I'D NEED SOMETHING MORE THAN *MOTIVE* TO FIGURE OUT WHO WAS BEHIND THAT WHEEL.

LIKE SOME HARD *EVIDENCE*.

HAH. VERY FUNNY.

⇥SIGH⇤

THE VAN HAD LITTLE TO OFFER IN THE WAY OF... JUST ABOUT ANYTHING.

WELL, THERE WERE THE RODS.

WHAT ARE THESE FOR? CLOTHES?

A LAUNDRY VAN. DRY CLEANER, MAYBE?

HAD I UNCOVERED ANY **DRY-CLEANING** PLOTS LATELY?

NOT THAT I REMEMBERED, AND MY MEMORY WAS PRETTY GOOD.

ONE RULE OF DETECTIVE WORK IS TO USE **ALL** YOUR SENSES, ESPECIALLY WHEN YOU LACK **VISIBLE** CLUES.

DRY CLEANING HAS A PARTICULAR SMELL.

≥SNIFF!≤
≥SNIFF!≤

AND THIS VAN **DIDN'T** SMELL LIKE DRY CLEANING.

AS THE VAN BACKED UP, I HEARD THE CRUNCHING OF LEAVES AND TWIGS UNDER THE TIRES.

THEN ALL WAS QUIET.

MUCH AS I HATED TO ADMIT IT, UNTIL SOMETHING ELSE HAPPENED, THERE WASN'T ANY MORE *DETECTING* I COULD DO.

LOOK, McGINNIS, I DON'T WANT TO INTERFERE IN ANY WAY WITH YOUR INVESTIGATION, BUT PLEASE BE AWARE THAT THIS BENEFIT RAISES MUCH-NEEDED FUNDS FOR NEARLY ALL RIVER HEIGHTS' CHARITIES.

YOU'RE RIGHT. FOR STARTERS, I'LL INTERVIEW PEOPLE ON THE SIDE, *QUIETLY*.

SHOULDN'T WE TELL CHIEF McGINNIS ABOUT OUR SUSPICIONS OF DEIRDRE?

NOT WITHOUT EVIDENCE. EVEN I HARDLY BELIEVE IT.

AT LEAST THE GIRLS WERE THINKING LIKE DETECTIVES. SORT OF.

PERSONALLY, I MIGHT HAVE CONSULTED THE CHIEF, AT THAT POINT.

MEANWHILE, DEIRDRE WAS LAVISHING IN WHAT WAS USUALLY AN IMPOSSIBLE DREAM... ATTENTION FROM NED.

KNOCK KNOCK

GO AWAY! UM... I MEAN... WHAT IS IT?

EXCUSE ME, KITTEN, BUT I NEED TO SPEAK WITH NED PRIVATELY A MINUTE.

NO! DOES HE HAVE TO GO?

SORRY, SWEETIE, IT'S IMPORTANT.

AND I'M NOT?

FINE, THEN! DON'T LEAVE ME ALONE TOO LONG, NED, I MAY DO SOMETHING *DRASTIC*.

I THINK NED LEFT. WHAT DO WE DO NOW?

MAYBE TRY TO JIMMY THE OTHER DOOR! LUCKILY, DEEDEE'S TOO PREOCCUPIED TO WORRY ABOUT HER CLOSET RIGHT NOW!

OR NOT! ACK!

I *THOUGHT* I HEARD RATS IN THERE. AND I WAS RIGHT! BIG RATS.

ONLY ONE OF THE RATS IS *MISSING*?! WHERE'S YOUR EVIL MISTRESS, NANCY DREW?

YOU TELL *US*! WHAT DO YOU KNOW ABOUT A WHITE VAN?

DID ONE OF YOUR PANDERING *PALS* SNATCH NANCY SO NO ONE WOULD SEE YOU HAVE THE SAME DRESS?

SUDDENLY, I WAS SENT FLYING BACKWARDS AGAIN. THE VAN WAS PULLING OUT, *FAST*.

VROOOM

HEY, DIDN'T THOSE CREEPS SAY SOMETHING ABOUT A WHITE VAN?

SCREEECH

THE DOOR OPENED FOR TWO SECONDS. I DIDN'T EVEN HAVE TIME TO STAND UP, MUCH LESS TRY AND ESCAPE.

AEEEIIIIK! DADDY! NED! HELP!

CHAPTER THREE: PERMANENT MESS

SHE SURE RAN HOT AND COLD. BUT NOT EVERYONE WAS AS USED TO THIS SORT OF THING AS I WAS.

I'D SUGGEST YOU KEEP YOUR CELL PHONES ON IN CASE THE GIRLS ARE TRYING TO REACH YOU.

OR THEIR KIDNAPPERS! I DON'T UNDERSTAND WHY NO ONE'S CALLED TO DEMAND MONEY.

UNLESS WE WERE RIGHT ABOUT IT BEING *REVENGE* AND DEIRDRE JUST HAD HERSELF KIDNAPPED TO AVOID *SUSPICION*.

DEIRDRE?!

GOT TO ADMIT... SHE IS THE MOST *LIKELY* SUSPECT.

SHE HAD MOTIVE...

AND IF YOU LEFT DEIRDRE ALONE FOR JUST FIVE MINUTES SHE HAD THE *OPPORTUNITY* TO CALL ONE OF HER HANGERS-ON TO PULL THIS PRANK FOR HER.

TRYING TO FILL THE DETECTIVE VOID, HUH, GIRLS?

IT'S A *BIG* VOID.

HMM. DEIRDRE AS THE CULPRIT IS A SCENARIO I'D LIKE TO BELIEVE.

BUT, ANGRY AS DEIRDRE IS, I DON'T THINK SHE'D HURT NANCY.

WHO SAID DEIRDRE'S *HURTING* NANCY?

YOU REALLY THINK THIS IS GOING TO...

CLICK

...WOOOORK!

WITH THE VAN RATTLING ALONG THE DIRT ROAD SO LOUDLY, THE DRIVER PROBABLY DIDN'T EVEN HEAR THE DOOR OPEN.

BUT I WASN'T GOING TO WAIT AROUND TO FIND OUT.

C'MON!

AHHHH! I TORE MY DRESS. NOT THAT I'LL EVER WEAR IT AGAIN! I WONDER HOW MANY THAT *HAS-BEEN* DESIGNER *MADE!*

SHHH!

BUT, I WAS *GLAD* SHE'D SAID IT.

THAT WAS IT. THE CONNECTION. THE ONLY REASON ANYONE WOULD HAVE TO SNATCH *BOTH* OF US ON THAT PARTICULAR NIGHT.

DEIRDRE WAS ONLY SLIGHTLY COMFORTED WHEN I PROMISED TO TRY AND ARRANGE IT SO NO ONE *ELSE* WOULD SEE US.

BUT, HER FEET HURT AND SHE NEVER HAD MUCH PATIENCE FOR MY SLEUTHING.

WHICH I CAN CERTAINLY UNDERSTAND. POKING AROUND DARK BASEMENTS ISN'T *EVERYONE'S* THING, AND SHE'D ALREADY HAD WHAT COUNTED FOR A ROUGH NIGHT IN HER LIFE.

NOW, IF WE'RE LUCKY I'LL FIND A...

FLASHLIGHT?

THEN AGAIN, LIKE I SAID, PEOPLE CAN SURPRISE YOU SOMETIMES.

SHINE IT HERE A MINUTE AND WE'LL DARKEN THE STAGE FOR OUR ENTRANCE.

WHAT'S WITH THE DRAMA?

OH, MY!? THE LIGHTS!? CALM DOWN, EVERYONE PLEASE! I'LL GO CHECK MYSELF!

TRUST ME DEIRDRE, FOR JUST A FEW *SECONDS* MORE. NOW, LET'S GET UPSTAIRS!

OKAY, SO THINGS DIDN'T WORK OUT *EXACTLY* THE WAY I PLANNED! I GUESS THE STAIRS TO THE BASEMENT WERE CLOSER TO THE PARTY THAN I THOUGHT!

≒GASP≒!

AHHHH!

WE WERE *BUSTED* JUST AS WE REACHED THE KITCHEN.

MADAM, THE POWER OUTAGE SET OFF THE ALARM. THE POLICE ARE HERE.

BRING THEM HERE QUICKLY, RODERICK, *WITHOUT* UPSETTING OUR GUESTS MORE THAN THEY ALREADY ARE.

THEY'LL DEAL WITH OUR DRESS-STEALING PARTY CRASHERS! AND FOR HEAVEN'S SAKE, GET THE LIGHTS BACK ON!

MAY I ASK WHAT YOU PAID FOR THAT DRESS, MRS. FARGO?

NOT THAT IT'S ANY OF YOUR BUSINESS, BUT *EMMA GRADY* AND HER ASSISTANT ARE COMING BY AFTER THE PARTY TO COLLECT A *FORTUNE* FOR THIS DRESS... WHICH SHE CLAIMED WAS ONE OF A KIND!!

BINGO.

OH, NOW I GET IT! *YOU* KIDNAPPED US JUST SO YOU COULD BE THE ONLY ONE IN TOWN WEARING THE DRESS!

NO, DEIRDRE. THAT'S *NOT* IT.

SHE HAD A GOOD MEMORY AND A KNACK FOR FINDING FLASHLIGHTS, BUT DEIRDRE STILL WASN'T AN ACE DETECTIVE.

I WAITED FOR EVERYONE TO ARRIVE BEFORE LAUNCHING INTO MY FAMOUS GIRL-DETECTIVE-EXPLAINS-ALL MODE.

MY PALS WERE ON THE RIGHT TRACK ABOUT THE WHY OF THE CRIME – WE WERE KIDNAPPED BECAUSE OF THE DRESSES – BUT A COUPLE MILES OFF ON THE WHO.

SEE, AFTER TRYING ON EVERY DRESS EMMA HAD, JANE FARGO FINALLY PICKED THE SAME DRESS DEIRDRE AND I HAD ALREADY BOUGHT.

WITH EMMA'S SHOP NOT DOING WELL, SHE HAD TO CHARGE JANE FARGO A FORTUNE FOR WHATEVER SHE BOUGHT, SO SHE LIED, SAYING IT WAS ONE-OF-A-KIND.

BUT, WHEN JANE INSISTED ON PAYING HER ONLY AFTER THE PARTY, EMMA HAD TO MAKE SURE NO ONE SAW US WEARING THE SAME DRESS UNTIL SHE HAD THE CASH.

SO...

WE WEREN'T GOING TO HURT YOU. WE PLANNED TO LET YOU GO AS SOON AS WE HAD THE MONEY. I... I NEVER DREAMED WE'D BE CAUGHT.

BUT HANNAH'S NOT THE SORT TO BACK DOWN, EVEN WHEN AFRAID, ESPECIALLY IF SHE'S *WORRIED* ABOUT ME.

I'VE ALWAYS *ADMIRED* THAT ABOUT HER...

...EVEN IF, AS THEY SAY, DISCRETION IS SOMETIMES THE BETTER PART OF VALOR.

WHICH MEANS, BASICALLY, SOMETIMES YOU SHOULD *LOOK* VERY CAREFULLY BEFORE YOU *LEAP*.

DON'T MISS NANCY DREW GRAPHIC NOVEL # 13 – "DOGGONE TOWN"

THE HARDY BOYS®

Eye a mystery...

Read NANCY DREW
girl detective™

WATCH OUT FOR PAPERCUTZ

If this is your very first Papercutz graphic novel, then allow me, Jim Salicrup, your humble and lovable Editor-in-Chief, to welcome you to the Papercutz Backpages where we check out what's happening in the ever-expanding Papercutz Universe! If you're a long-time Papercutz fan, then welcome back, friend!

Things really have been popping at Papercutz! In the last few editions of the Backpages we've announced new titles such as TALES FROM THE CRYPT, CLASSICS ILLUSTRATED, and CLASSICS ILLUSTRATED DELUXE. Well, guess what? The tradition continues, and we're announcing yet another addition to our line-up of blockbuster titles. So, what is our latest and greatest title? We'll give you just one hint -- the stars of the next Papercutz graphic novel series just happen to be the biggest, most exciting line of constructible action figures ever created! That's right -- BIONICLE is coming! Check out the power-packed preview pages ahead!

Before I run out of room, let me say that we're always interested in what you think! Are there characters, TV shows, movies, books, videogames, you-name-it, that you'd like to see Papercutz turn into graphic novels? Don't be shy, let's us know! You can contact me at salicrup@papercutz.com or Jim Salicrup, PAPERCUTZ, 40 Exchange Place, Ste. 1308, New York, NY 10005 and let us know how we're doing. After all, we want you to be as excited about Papercutz as we are!

Thanks,

Jim

EDITOR-IN-CHIEF

Caricature drawn by Steve Brodner at the MoCCA Art Fest.

TWO DOZEN TEEN DETECTIVE
GRAPHIC NOVELS NOW IN PRINT!

You know, while it's exciting to be adding so many new titles, we don't want anyone to think we've forgotten any of our previous Papercutz publications! For example, can you believe there are now two dozen all-new, full-color graphic novels starring America's favorite teen sleuths?! In fact, let's check out what's happening in the 12th volumes of both NANCY DREW and HARDY BOYS...

Writers Stefan Petrucha and Sarah Kinney and artists Sho Murase and Carlos Jose Guzman present Nancy's latest case, "Dress Reversal." After showing up at River Height's social event of the

year, in the identical dress as the party's hostess, Deirdre Shannon, things get worse for Nancy when she's suddenly kidnapped! That leaves Bess, George, and Ned to solve the mystery of the missing Girl Detective.

Meanwhile, writer Scot Lobdell, and artist Paulo Henrique Marcondes have sent Frank and Joe Hardy way out West to the "Dude Ranch O' Death!" (You'd think people would think twice before going there, right?) When kids turn up missing at a "tough love" camp for troubled teens, A.T.A.C. sends the Undercover Brothers in to investigate. What they find will surprise you!

Behold. . .

BIONICLE ®

At the start of the new millennium,

a new line of toys from Lego made their dramatic debut. Originally released in six color-coded canisters, each containing a constructible, fully-poseable, articulated character, BIONICLE was an instant hit!

The BIONICLE figures were incredibly intriguing. With their exotic names hinting at a complex history, fans were curious to discover more about these captivating characters. Even now, over six years later, there are still many unanswered questions surrounding every facet of the ever-expanding BIONICLE universe.

A comicbook, written by leading BIONICLE expert and author of most of the BIONICLE novels Greg Farshtey, was created by DC Comics and given away to members of the BIONICLE fan club. The action-packed comics revealed much about these mysterious biomechanical (part biological, part mechanical) beings and the world they inhabited. A world filled with many races, most prominent being the Matoran. A world once protected millennia ago by a Great Spirit known as Mata Nui, who has fallen asleep. A world that has begun to decay as its inhabitants must defend themselves from the evil forces of Makuta.

These early comics are incredibly hard-to-find, and many new BIONICLE fans have never seen these all-important early chapters in this epic science fantasy. But soon, those comics will be collected as the first two volumes in the Papercutz series of BIONICLE graphic novels.

In the following pages, enjoy a special preview of BIONICLE graphic novel #1...

In TALES FROM THE CRYPT graphic novel #1 "Ghouls Gone Wild!" Tommy expresses what most action figure fans think.

FULL-COLOR GRAPHIC NOVEL

BIONICLE

#1: RISE OF THE TOA NUVA

GREG FARSHTEY   RICHARD BENNETT   RANDY ELLIOTT

HOW IT ALL BEGAN...

PAPERCUTZ

LEGO

DON'T MISS BIONICLE GRAPHIC NOVEL #1 "RISE OF THE TOA NUVA"

A SPECIAL EXCLUSIVE

NANCY DREW

girl detective

BONUS FEATURE!

A long time ago, young Jim Salicrup, and even younger Stefan Petrucha, would talk about writing and drawing comics. They even worked on writing and drawing their own comics. Not that long ago, Jim got to edit a series X-Files comics written by Stefan. Even more recently, Jim asked his childhood friend to write the all-new Papercutz graphic novel series, NANCY DREW, and he agreed. And very recently, Stefan's wife Sarah Kinney, who's a writer as well, started helping him write NANCY DREW.

Last year, Mrs. Schreiber's third grade class had a very special project -- create a Nancy Drew comic. What's even more amazing is that Margo Kinney-Petrucha, daughter of Stefan and Sarah, was a member of that class. While all the students did wonderful work, we just had to show you Margot's terrific tale of everyone's favorite Girl Detective. So without further ado, check out this awesome artistic debut!

I couldn't believe the train had made a turn by itself. I still worried about how much I'll have to pay for that broken stop lever.